Swift Fox
All Along

Story by
Rebecca Thomas

Pictures by
Maya McKibbin

annick press
toronto • berkeley

This book is dedicated to every Indigenous kid and adult who had to seek out where they came from. It was in you all along.

—R.T.

If you have felt like you have not been enough, or are uncomfortable living out who you feel to be your true self, this is for you. Embrace yourself and who you are! It's your right! Thank you everyone in my life who has seen me for who I am and to myself for continuing to be.

—M.M.

Swift Fox's belly
fills with butterflies.

Usually, if her dad visits,
they go for ice cream or to the park.

Most of the time her big sister comes, too.

But not today.

Today, he's taking her on a long drive to a place she's never been before.
Mom says she's old enough now.

"Are you excited?" her dad asks.
"You're going to meet your aunties and uncles, cousins too! Today you're going to learn how to be Mi'kmaq."

Dad says he's proud to be Mi'kmaq.
But what does it mean?

Swift Fox eyes the red bundle in the
back seat. "What's Mi'kmaq?"

"It's who you are! From your eyes to
your toes. It's what's inside you."

"It's how you walk, talk, and think." Her father winks.

Swift Fox already knows how to walk and talk. And how does she "think Mi'kmaq"?

The butterflies in her belly get bigger.

Before long, her dad pulls into a driveway. "We're here!"

Swift Fox swallows hard to keep the butterflies
from getting out. "Dad, I don't want to go in. I'm scared."

"It's okay, Swift Fox, it's who you are!
They're your family. They're a part of you."

"What if they don't like me?"

"Wha-sa-matta-with-ya, child?
Don't worry! It'll be fine."

Before she can say anything else her dad
nudges her into the house.

Swift Fox looks around the room.

She notices a red bundle like
the one her dad has in his car.
She wonders what's in it.

A woman who looks like her dad walks over.
"Look at you, Nsim. My niece. Those freckles sure are cute!"

All the eyes in the room turn to her. Swift Fox's cheeks get hot.
Her heart beats faster. The butterflies want out.

"We were just about to smudge," a man says,
taking a braid of grass from the red bundle.

"Swift Fox, this is your uncle." Her dad smiles. "Go on. He's waiting."

The butterflies in her tummy grow into birds.

"But I don't know how,"
Swift Fox whispers.

"Sure you do!' Her dad nudges
her shoulder. "It's who you are."

Suddenly, Swift Fox's cheeks feel wet.
A whine escapes her throat.

"If it's inside me, why can't I find it?"

Swift Fox covers her
tear-stained freckles
and runs out the door.

She spies a space under
the porch and crawls in.

"I can't believe she didn't know how to smudge," one cousin says.

"Everybody knows how," says another.

"I'll race you to the store!"

Swift Fox listens to the voices of her new family drift out the window.

"Poor girl . . ."

"She'll come back when she's ready."

"I'm not coming back . . ." whispers Swift Fox.

She already has a sister. She doesn't need any more family!

Why didn't her dad just take her to the park!

Swift Fox picks at the bandage on her knee.

She studies the pebbles on the ground.

With her eyes, she traces the edges of the leaves.

Swift Fox listens to the wind rustling the trees—the same kind of trees that are in the park she goes to with her dad.

She notices a familiar smell drifting from the house.

It's the bread her dad makes in the frying pan!

Sometimes he puts raisins in it.
He always serves it with butter and molasses.

Swift Fox loves that bread.

Swift Fox hears another car pulling up to the house.

"Mom," a boy says, "I don't want to go inside.
I don't know them."

"Come on. It's time to meet your cousins."

The boy's mom walks up the stairs and into the house.

The boy has freckles just like her!

He looks like he has a belly full of butterflies, too.

"Who are you?" the boy asks.

"Swift Fox." She stands a little taller.
"Who are you?"

"Sully," he says.

Sully eyes her up and down.

Swift Fox feels her cheeks
get hot all over again.

Who is he anyway?

"What's that smell?"
He wrinkles his nose.

"It's the best bread in the world! My dad puts molasses and butter on it. It's so good!"

"Yeah? Then why aren't you in there eating it?"

Swift Fox hears her dad's laughter coming from the house.

She takes a big sigh. A few butterflies escape.

"You want to go try some?"

She starts to climb the stairs.

"Kwe! Look who came back!"
Her uncle smiles.

"I see you've met your cousin."
Her aunt gathers them both in a hug.

"Are you ready?"
asks her dad.

Swift Fox's dad takes the braid of grass and shows her what to do.

She leans in and pulls the smoke over her head, to her eyes, mouth, and heart.

She knows that smell.

Her butterflies fly away.

"I told you she'd figure it out," one of the cousins whispers.

Swift Fox stops in front of Sully.

He hesitates and looks at her.

"It's okay," she says. "It's inside of you.
Sometimes it's just hard to find."

Author's Note

I grew up off-reserve. My parents separated when I was very young. I lived with my mom, while my dad lived in different cities and countries. I didn't get to see him very much as a child, and I didn't meet his relatives until I was a little bit older and able to travel away from home. The first time I met my dad's side of the family, I was nervous because they were strangers and I wasn't sure if they were going to accept me.

Like many Mi'kmaq people his age, my father attended the Shubenacadie Residential School. Over 1,000 Indigenous children attended that particular school over its 37-year life span. My father was the same age when he was separated from his family as I was when I visited the reserve for the first time. He lost his language and much of his culture, but not his spirit. He didn't teach me a lot of things about my culture because he either couldn't remember or didn't know how to connect with me. I was, and still am, nervous when I do any kind of ceremony, like smudging or sweats. I'm afraid I'm going to do it wrong even though I now know what to do.

With everything my dad experienced, he managed to connect me and my siblings to an identity in hopes we would latch onto it. I'm very proud of who I am. I'm learning to walk, talk, and think a little more Mi'kmaq with each passing year.

Rebecca Thomas

Edited by Mary Beth Leatherdale
Cover art by Maya McKibbin, designed by Paul Covello
Interior design by Paul Covello

Annick Press Ltd.

We acknowledge the support of the Canada Council for the Arts and the Ontario Arts Council, and the participation of the Government of Canada/la participation du gouvernement du Canada for our publishing activities.

Canada ☀

ONTARIO ARTS COUNCIL
CONSEIL DES ARTS DE L'ONTARIO
an Ontario government agency
un organisme du gouvernement de l'Ontario

Library and Archives Canada Cataloguing in Publication

Title: Swift Fox all along / story by Rebecca Thomas ; pictures by Maya McKibbin.
Names: Thomas, Rebecca (Poet), author. | McKibbin, Maya, 1995- illustrator.
Identifiers: Canadiana (print) 20200193996 | Canadiana (ebook) 20200194046 | ISBN 9781773214481
    (hardcover) | ISBN 9781773214511 (PDF) | ISBN 9781773214498 (HTML) | ISBN 9781773214504 (Kindle
Classification: LCC PS8639.H5875 L66 2020 | DDC jC813/.6—dc23

Published in the U.S.A. by Annick Press (U.S.) Ltd.
Distributed in Canada by University of Toronto Press.
Distributed in the U.S.A. by Publishers Group West.

Printed in China

annickpress.com

mkchibs.com

Also available as an e-book. Please visit annickpress.com/ebooks for more details.